SHINE

SARAH ASUQUO

ILLUSTRATED BY FLORELLE BOHI

Matador
9 Priory Business Park,
Wistow Road, Kibworth Beauchamp,
Leicestershire. LE8 0RX
Tel: 0116 279 2299
Email: books@troubador.co.uk
Web: www.troubador.co.uk/matador
Twitter: @matadorbooks

ISBN 978 1789017 151

British Library Cataloguing in Publication Data.
A catalogue record for this book is available from the British Library.

Typeset in 24pt Ten Oldstyle by Troubador Publishing Ltd, Leicester, UK

Matador is an imprint of Troubador Publishing Ltd

Dedicated to my nephews, Malachi and Ethan, and my nieces, Eliora and 'Baby M'. Always let your light shine. With special thanks to my mother and father; your sacrifices and love will forever be appreciated.

Sarah Asuquo

'Bye Mum!' yelled Kai, as he briskly closed the car door and raced towards the school gates, filled with excitement. It was the first day of school after the summer holiday and Kai could not wait to see his friends.

'Have a good day, I'll see you later,' replied his mother, as she smiled and watched her thrilled son.

However, Kai's journey home was very different to the cheerful ride in the morning.

'How was your first day back at school?' his mother asked, with an expression of concern on her face. Kai stared sadly through his window and did not respond.

After some minutes had passed, Kai sighed deeply and said, *'We built a den at school today, for kids to hide, explore and play. I thought the den was built for all; they said, "No Kai, you're too tall." I wish that I was smaller, I wish I wasn't tall. Then I could fit inside the den like Tom and Sam and Paul.'*

Kai's mother parked the car, held his hand and said, '*Be proud my son that you are tall, stand as high as you can be. For you can see far and beyond what other children see. Everyone is different, my son, be true to you. Within us all is a special light, will you let yours shine through?*' Kai simply nodded.

The next evening, whilst eating dinner, Kai's father noticed that his son was unusually quiet.

'How was your day, Kai?' he asked, placing his hand on Kai's shoulder.

Kai briefly paused and replied, '*When changing for P.E. today, I wore my boots, so I could play, but just as I had put them on, Jack laughed and said, "Your feet are long." I wish my feet were not so big, I wish that they were small. Then I'd fit in, like Jack and Jim and play with them at school.*'

Kai's father was disappointed to hear that his son had been teased at school. He said, '*Be proud my son of your large feet, for you should not forget, that with your feet you'll march and leap with strength in every step. Everyone is different, my son, be true to you. Within us all is a special light, will you let yours shine through?*' Kai simply nodded.

The following night, Kai could not sleep; he was thinking about his day. Kai's mother noticed that the light was on in his bedroom, so she opened the door and asked him why he was still awake. With a gentle breath, Kai answered.

'At lunchtime in the dinner hall, whilst eating apple pie, Jack pointed and then asked me, "What's that under your eye?" It's just a scar, I told him, I fell when I was small. He laughed and said, "That's strange," and led the laughter of them all. I wish that I was perfect, I wish I had no scars, then I'd be like my friends at school, I'd be regular.'

Kai's mother realised that her son had an important lesson to learn. The time felt right and with a calm voice she said, '*Be proud my son of all your scars, don't be ashamed or hide. They show you've learned and overcome, they add to your own shine.*'

She pulled open Kai's curtains, revealing the bright night sky and asked him to stand beside her.

'*Look up at the stars at night, they twinkle in the sky. Then watch the moonlight up above the clouds, so very high. Can you compare the stars and moon and say that one is best? They both shine in the sky each night so beautifully as we rest. Everyone is different, my son, be true to you. Within us all is a special light, will you let yours shine through?*' Kai firmly nodded.

Kai's mother tucked him into bed, kissed his forehead and wished him a good night. Kai began to think about what his mother and father had said to him over the last three days. He realised that the things that make him different are the things that make him special.

'*I choose to use all the things that make me who I am and make sure that I shine my light as brightly as I can.*'

The next day at playtime, Kai noticed that his friend Sam was upset and asked him what was wrong.

With tears in his eyes, Sam said, '*I went out to the playground to play basketball, but everybody laughed at me. Jack said I was too small. I wish that I was taller, I wish I was like you. Then I could hop and leap and jump like other children do.*'

Kai told Sam what he had learned about the stars and the moon. He said, *'You can shine your special light, just the way you are. You move so quickly when you play, just like a shooting star. With my height and your speed, we'll make a perfect team. I've got an excellent idea, Sam you can play with me!'*

Kai and Sam played basketball together and were enjoying themselves so much that they did not notice the other children in their class watching them in admiration. Kai leaped and jumped, shooting the ball through the hoop repeatedly. Whilst Sam sped across the playground, bouncing the ball so skilfully. The children cheered and clapped so loudly that the teachers upstairs could hear them!

Jack realised that he had been unkind and wanted to make things right. He slowly approached the two boys and said, '*Hello Kai and Sam, you both play really well. I'm sorry that I laughed at you... may I play as well?*'

Kai and Sam looked at each other and smiled with great delight...

'Of course,' said Kai, 'we all can shine, if we just unite.'

ILLUSTRATOR'S MESSAGE

With thanks to my mum, Jean Bohi, for encouraging me to pursue my artistic talent. In loving memory of my dad, Antione Bohi, for giving me the confidence to believe in myself.

Florelle Bohi